Fritz and the Beautiful Horses

Jan Brett

1987

Fritz and the Beautiful Horses

Written and Illustrated by

Jan Brett

Houghton Mifflin Company Boston

for my mother and father

Library of Congress Cataloging in Publication Data
Bret, Jan, 1949—
    Fritz and the beautiful horses.
    SUMMARY: Fritz, a pony excluded from the group of
beautiful horses within the walled city, becomes a hero
when he rescues the children of the city.
    [1. Ponies—Fiction.   2. Horses—Fiction]
I. Title.
PZ7.B7559Fr   [Fic]   80-26915
ISBN 0-395-30850-X

Copyright ©1981 by Jan Brett

All rights reserved. No part of this work may be reproduced or transmitted in any
form or by any means, electronic or mechanical, including photocopying and
recording, or by any information storage or retrieval system, except as may be
expressly permitted by the 1976 Copyright Act or in writing from the publisher.
Requests for permission should be addressed in writing to Houghton Mifflin
Company, 2 Park Street, Boston, Massachusetts 02108.
Printed in the United States of America.

H 10 9 8 7 6 5 4 3

Once there was a walled city known for its beautiful horses.

There were magnificent jumpers, splendid chargers, and elegant parade horses.

The citizens were so proud of these horses that it was decreed that only the most beautiful would be allowed in the city. All others would have to stay outside.

One of these was a pony named Fritz.

Fritz was not beautiful. He had a long, tangled mane, whiskers on
his muzzle, and short legs. But Fritz was very gentle and kind.
He was sure-footed and always willing to work.

Day after day, Fritz watched the beautiful horses. Some had braided
manes and tails, and carried lovely ladies. Others had glossy
coats and pulled grand carriages.

Most of all he watched the children's horses.

"I wonder why the children look so frightened?" he thought.

The children were afraid. They didn't like their horses prancing and leaping. It made them very difficult to ride.

As Fritz watched he thought, "I would like a child to ride me."
But no one ever noticed Fritz.

One day he climbed up to the road leading to the walled city.
He tried to take long, graceful strides. He pranced and curved his
neck. He threw his tail into the air.

The citizens stared at Fritz and then they began to laugh.
"Look at that silly horse," they said.

Then the lovely ladies and the magnificent gentlemen galloped away
toward the walled city. The children followed reluctantly behind.
"I guess I do look silly," thought Fritz and he hung his head in despair.

Fritz listened to the citizens as they galloped their horses faster and faster. He heard their loud cheers as they rode onto the bridge to the walled city.

All of a sudden he heard a loud SNAP. The bridge was breaking under
the weight of the horses' pounding hooves.

Fritz saw a large crack appear in the middle of the bridge.

The citizens were on one side and the children were on the other.

"You'll have to cross through the river," cried the citizens.

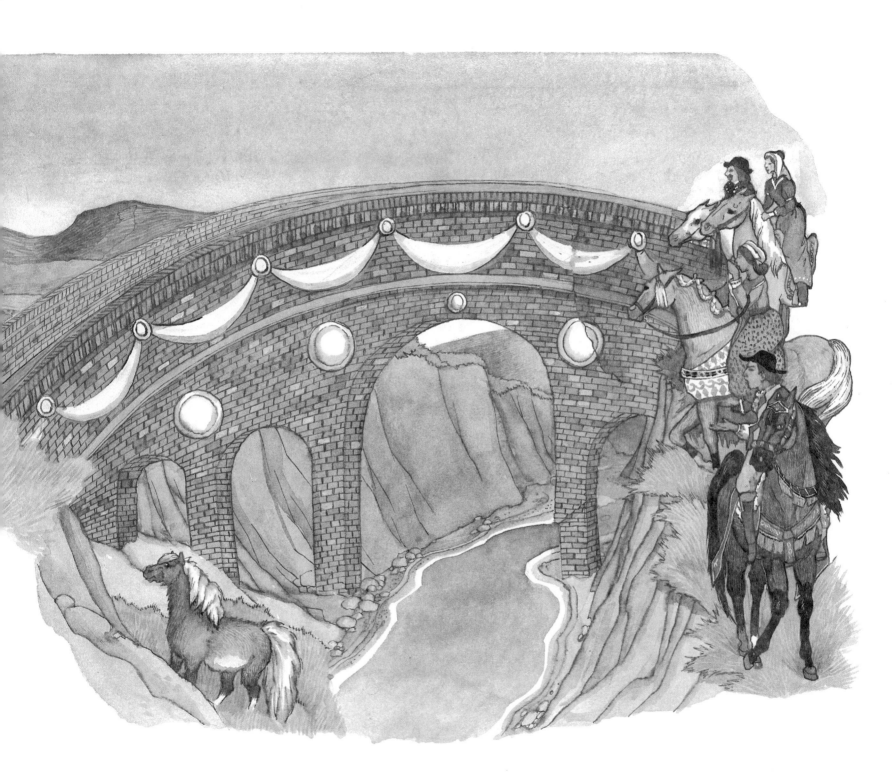

But the children wouldn't move.

"My horse might shy and buck," said one.

"My horse might leap and stumble," said another.

"We might fall off," they all cried together.

"Stay where you are," shouted the citizens. "We will come and get you."

But their horses wouldn't move.

"This hill is much too steep," thought one horse.

"My lovely mane might get tangled in the bushes," thought another.

"We certainly don't want to get wet," all the horses agreed.

Everyone wondered what to do. Then they noticed Fritz.

Fritz carefully climbed to where the children waited.

Fritz was not beautiful, but he was gentle and kind. He was sure-footed and always willing to work. The children were not afraid to ride him.

One by one Fritz carried the children carefully down the steep hill.
He calmly stepped through the river from rock to rock and
up the other side.

He finally carried all the children to the walled city.

A great cheer went up from the citizens.

The lovely ladies cried, "Hurray for the sure-footed pony!"

The gentlemen said, "How kind and dependable he is!"

And the children exclaimed, "We didn't fall off!"
So Fritz was given a special place in the walled city.
All the children cared for him and became his friends.

From that day on, the walled city was known for its beautiful horses and its very dependable pony.